My Grandpa and Mr Alzheimer

A fairy tale for the young and the old

ISBN: 978-93-55463-25-8
eISBN: 978-93-55463-26-5

Publisher: **Pharos Books (P) Ltd.**
Plot No.-55, Main Mother Dairy Road
Pandav Nagar, East Delhi-110092 (India)
Phone: +014049995474
WhatsApp: +014049995474
E-mail: sales@pharosbooks.in
Website: www.pharosbooks.in
Edition: 2022

My Grandpa and Mr. Alzheimer
Author: Epi Zeggou

Epi Zeggou

My Grandpa and Mr Alzheimer

A fairy tale for the young and the old

Pharos Books

To my children

Granddad

A sweet, tender man who loves spending his time with his three grandchildren, but who is, unfortunately, affected by a form of dementia, which makes the whole family sad.

Grandmom

The sweet and lovely Grandma who patiently takes care of the Grandpa.

Gerasimos

The oldest of the three grandchildren, agonizing over his Granddad's condition, decides to write a letter to him explaining how he and the rest of the family are feeling.

Hermione and Beatrice
The two granddaughters of the family who are very close to the Granddad and who love his sweet hugs and the fairytales he is telling them. The girls, without understanding Granddad's serious disease, imitate his behaviour as they think that is funny and cheeky. Their jokes always create problems and unpredictable situations within the family.

Mr. Alzheimer
The German psychiatrist and neuropathologist Alois Alzheimer who, in 1906, identified the broadly known Alzheimer disease, named after him.

Tiny Human Cells
The nervous cells that live and work in the brain and inside the human body. They gather pictures and information from the outside world, store them in the brain, and carry instructions from the brain to the various organs of the body which then perform them.

Dear Grandpa

I decided to write to you, as the oldest of your grandchildren, to tell you how Hermione, Beatrice and I feel about all the things that are happening lately.

I feel so strange; all of us feel the same. It is so difficult to understand what is happening to you.

Sometimes, when you come home, you open your arms and we run to you for a hug.

You talk to us, you caress our hair, you tell us fairytales and sing songs, but, suddenly, you get up and you rush out, leaving the room empty.

Other times, though, you get angry and you start shouting so loudly that you scare the life out of us.

Luckily your anger does not last long.

The strangest thing, though is that when we ask you what made you so angry, you do not even remember it.

And there are so many other things that you do not remember, Grandpa.

Very often you ask us the same questions repeatedly.

We answer them, and you very quickly forget our answers. And you ask us the same thing. Again.

Ah, Grandpa, how many times do I have to I tell you how old I am and which grade I am in at school?

And how is it possible that you do not remember my name and who I am?

I wonder if you think that it is funny to call me by different names.

How can you forget someone that you love so much? How can that happen?

Yesterday, at noon, suddenly you opened the door and without saying anything to anyone, you left. We did not notice at first that you had gone as your clothes and shoes were in their usual place.

It was getting dark, and you did not show up. We got really worried and we went out to look for you. We looked in every possible place that you could have been.

Finally, after a long time, Daddy found you in the park. You were wandering around in your pajamas and slippers. You, who are always well dressed and well presented.

How is that possible? Can you please explain it to me?

Did you just forget to get dressed?

Or were you in a rush to go somewhere?

And then, why did you not come back home? Didn't you get hungry? Were your feet not hurting after walking for so many hours?

And when you and Daddy returned, you were shouting that you do not want to go back home, to your children and wife! Why?

Grandpa, this is your home. Don't you remember it?

Grandma was very worried, so she called your doctor at home.

He examined you for a long time and then he said a lot of things that I did not understand. He also said a very strange word: "Alzheimer's".

Grandma was listening to him and she burst into tears. Why?

Mom, however, explained to us that Alzheimer was a famous doctor who discovered one of the illnesses that slowly destroys the brain. And she told us that you are suffering from an illness like that.

How is it possible that there is no medicine to help you to get well? I want you so much to be healed. I want you to be able to take me for a walk again.

I dream of you telling us stories and fairytales, that you are bringing us ice cream, that we play and laugh all together, as we used to do before you got sick.

Grandpa, I so much miss us sitting together and talking. And there are so many things that I need to tell you, such as my dream last night about the two of us sitting in your bedroom.

While we were chatting, you looked at me and you said: “Oh boy, every day I am getting older, I forget things more and more often, I get lost in the streets, I can hardly recognise people around me. What am I going to do from now on?” And you were so sad, Grandpa.

I then held your face with my hands; I touched my forehead to yours, looked at you and said, “Grandpa, do not worry about it. I am here for you, I will always look after you, I will always help you to find your way home and I will never leave you alone”.

And as I was looking deep into your eyes, something very strange happened: I became tiny and I started slipping inside your head, Grandpa, and guess who was waiting for me there? Mr. Alzheimer!

"You are very stressed over your Grandpa's situation, right?" he asked me.

"Of course; I worry about him a lot. I cannot understand what is happening to him, and I don't know what to do to help him. Mom said that Grandpa suffers from a disease, which destroys his mind. But I really don't understand how the mind can be destroyed. How is that possible?"

"Follow me," he said. "We will go for a walk into your Grandpa's head and I will show you how it works. We will see the world the same way that your Grandpa does. You are quite young to understand everything, but I will do my best to explain some things as simply as I can. Are you coming?" he asked.

"Yes, of course I am," I told him. Without having second thoughts, I followed him.

"Well, let's agree to call the mind by its more scientific name, which is brain, ok?" Mr. Alzheimer asked me.

"Sure, we will call it brain," I answered in my most formal attitude.

I was fascinated by this tour inside the mind – oops - inside the brain, I meant to say – I had so many things to learn from this famous doctor!

"Think of the brain as a very large block of flats. In each block, there are countless flats inside, in which the most advanced computers exist. In these computers, many tiny little humans live and work - the nerve cells," Mr. Alzheimer said in a very serious manner.

"How many of these tiny human cells are there? And what is their job?" I asked, full of curiosity.

"Oh, they are countless. There might even be one hundred billion!" he said.

"One hundred billion tiny human cells? That many? How do they fit in the brain? Do they not get squashed? And how do they work? What exactly is their function? Will you explain it to me?" I asked persistently.

"The nerve cells are minute, so they fit well in the brain and they are not constricted at all. I will now explain how they work: they gather information and images from the world outside to transfer and store on the computers which are located inside the brain flats."

"What kind of information?" I asked again.

"When you see, for example, a very beautiful rose, the nerve cells transfer to the brain the information that what it sees is a beautiful flower that smells good and is called a rose, that it has thorns which prick, and that it cannot be eaten," said Mr. Alzheimer.

"And how do the nerve cells gather all this information?"

Mr. Alzheimer smiled and said: "That's an excellent question. They gather this information in a very simple way, just by asking." Before I could say anything, he carried on. "For example, when you first see a beautiful flower, you will ask about it and someone older will tell you what it is and what it is called. He or she will ask you to smell it and will tell you to be careful not to be pierced by its thorns. And, of course, you will be told that humans do not eat flowers."

I was very curious to learn more. "And how is this information transferred inside humans?" I asked.

"Well, nerve cells communicate with each other by sending messages."

"Do you mean that these tiny human cells communicate with each other by sending text messages? Do they have mobile phones? They must be the tiniest phones in the world..."

"No, they do not have mobile phones, but all information which is transferred from one nerve cell to the next happens in almost the same way that messages are transferred between the cell phones people use today. Every message reaches its destination and is stored in the appropriate computer located within the brain flats."

"And what's the point of storing the information there?"

"Because the next time you see a rose, the nerve cells will send a notification to the brain saying - "

"And why should the brain be notified?" I interrupted him.

"The brain should be notified because that is the only that way it is able to read and recognise the information that is stored in the computers."

"And only when the brain gets these notifications can it give the correct instructions?" I asked.

"Exactly," Mr. Alzheimer said and smiled.

"So, you are saying that all commands and instructions come from the brain?" I asked again.

"Exactly. Humans breathe, walk, talk, eat, sleep, laugh, dance, sing, cry, read, remember because our brain works and gives these commands. Without commands and instructions from the brain, nothing would work properly."

"So is the brain so important?" I asked again. "I could never imagine something like that. So, my Grandpa often forgets things or does not recognise places and people, because his brain does not get the right information and then it gives out the wrong instructions?"

"That's exactly what happens," Mr. Alzheimer replied.

"And why don't these tiny human cells send him messages with the right information?"

"Because sometimes the nerve cells are disabled and cannot carry the messages."

"And how does that happen? Why can't they carry the messages? What happens to them? Can you please explain it to me? It is really difficult to understand."

Mr. Alzheimer thought for a moment and then said: "In a nutshell, sometimes there are obstacles in the brain that do not let the nerve cells carry the messages."

"What kind of obstacles are these? Where do they come from? Could you please tell me more; I really don't get it."

"I will. Or even better, I will show you," he said. "Follow me."

He walked ahead in very long strides and I was running to keep up with him. We left behind the large buildings of the front part of the brain and, after walking for a while, we saw in front of us a building with a very strange shape. It was like a snail. Mr. Alzheimer insisted that it looked like a hippocampus, a strange little marine fish which is also called a sea horse.

He opened the front door of the building and we started descending a very narrow and cramped staircase.

Inside this strange building was the most sophisticated computer I had ever seen. It was enormous and had countless screens. It looked like a huge bookcase but on every shelf, instead of books, there were screens. Millions of screens!

Some screens were colourful, bright and full of images, while others were dark and colourless.

"Where are we?" I asked Mr. Alzheimer.

"We are at the place where all of the brain's information meets to create memories."

"And how are memories being made?" I asked again.

"When we meet someone, his or her image is transferred from the nerve cells to this computer. In the same computer the nerve cells transfer information about the person's name and about our relationship with them, whether they are our relatives, friends, or just people we know, along with much other information about them.

"Then, the nerve cells process and transfer this information to be stored in the computers located in the various flats of the brain.

"So, when we see this person again, the nerve cells notify the brain, the brain recognises the face and instructs us to say hello. The brain assures us that we know this person."

I spotted some screens that were out of order and I asked Mr. Alzheimer why they were not working.

"Because sometimes, due to different causes, the lights in the various buildings of the brain are broken and the nerve cells cannot work in the dark."

"Oh! I think I understand now! Is this what you meant before when you said that sometimes there are some obstacles in the brain that make it difficult for the tiny human cells to function?"

"Yes, you understand it very well now! The various obstacles stop the nerve cells who live and work here from doing anything, so the images that contain the memories disappear. This is the case here with the dark and empty screens. Therefore, the more the light fades, the harder it is for someone with a brain like that to recognise or remember his friends, his childhood, and his loved ones.

"However, sometimes it happens that you recognise things around you, as the lights flicker and blink before they completely fail. This happens because sometimes the nerve cells have enough light and can work, and some other times they are in the dark and cannot do anything."

At that moment, Hermione and Beatrice entered the room. I heard them talking loudly and I realised that they were there, but when I looked at them, I could not recognise their faces. They seemed different; I felt like I had never met them before in my life.

"You've probably been wrong," I said to Mr. Alzheimer very happily. "You see, Grandpa just needs to get a new pair of eyeglasses to improve his eyesight. He does not see us clearly, that's why he does not recognise us."

"My little boy, the problem is not with his eyesight," he answered. "There is nothing wrong with his eyeglasses. As I told you before, from here we can see everything in the same way that your Grandpa does. He is now seeing two little kids very clearly but the problem is that he cannot remember who they are. Do you know why? Because the nerve cells that carry the messages with the pictures and the names of the girls were plunged into darkness, so they never managed to send the information they had to. And without this information, your Grandpa is unable to remember and recognise the two girls that are in front of him."

I was desperately looking for an answer.

"If the lights fail in the computer room where the information about the rose is stored, then Grandpa will touch the rose without thinking and he will be pierced by its thorns, or even worse, he might want to taste it. And all this happens because the brain has not received the right information and will therefore send the wrong orders?"

"This is exactly what will happen," said Mr. Alzheimer.

"And what will happen next?" I asked. "Will all these lights ever work again? Will the tiny human cells be able to do their job?"

Mr. Alzheimer smiled sadly as he looked at me. He pushed up his monocle, which was slipping down, and he cleared his throat before saying something that I was not prepared to hear:

"Never again."

I was just about to burst into tears when I asked him: "What do you mean by never again?"

"I mean, that slowly, the same thing will happen in every building of your Grandpa's brain. The little lights will flicker but will eventually turn off forever. We do not know exactly when, but at some point, the lights in the room where all the information about food is stored, will switch off completely. And the brain then will no longer be able to send through the nerve cells a command to the body to chew and to swallow the food. So your Grandpa will not be able to eat. When the lights in the computer room where the words are stored switch off, your Grandpa will struggle to speak and express how he feels or ask you for something that he needs.

ROOM OF APPETITE
ROOM OF CALMNESS

I looked at him full of despair.

"And what do you do to save him from being lost to darkness? Nothing! This is not fair, Mr. Alzheimer," I said. "You are a doctor and you must find a way to cure my Grandpa."

"Dear Gerasimos, I am very old. Don't forget that I was a doctor for the past century and the only reason that I am here now is to help you understand what is going on in your Grandpa's brain. Unfortunately, there is nothing else that I can do. I want you to know that there are thousands of scientists around the world who work, day and night to find a treatment for your grandfather's illness."

I opened my eyes as wide as I could and I asked: "Really? So many scientists are trying to cure my Grandpa?"

"They are working hard not only for your Grandpa but for every grandfather, grandmother, and other people around the world who get sick and lose their memory."

"What do you mean by memory? What is that? You keep teaching me new words!"

"Hmmm! Let's say that memory is the human ability to recognise and remember everything important in someone's life," said Mr. Alzheimer.

"And why is this happening? Why do people lose their memory?"

"It is a disease, like all other diseases that people suffer from."

"What does disease mean? I have never heard this word before."

"Disease is the scientific name for the word 'illness'."

"Oh, ok, I get it! It is because of this disease that the lights in the flats of the brain break down? But where this disease comes from? How can someone get it?"

"That is complex to explain. In fact, it is not only one disease. There are various causes and multiple diseases that can lead a human being to the same condition as your Grandpa."

"Do you mean then that there are multiple reasons why people lose their memory?"

"Yes, there are many causes and it's quite difficult to analyse each of them separately. But what I can tell you is that none of these diseases can be transmitted. Whatever the reason your grandfather has lost his memory, you are not going to be infected. So, you can be close to your grandfather. Play with him, hug and kiss him, without being afraid that you will get the virus. This is not going to happen!"

"Phew! This is great news! I couldn't even dream of not seeing my Grandpa," I said. "But what will happen to my Grandpa? Can you please tell me if there is anything that we can do to help him?"

Mr. Alzheimer went silent for a few seconds.

"Just to love him," he said.

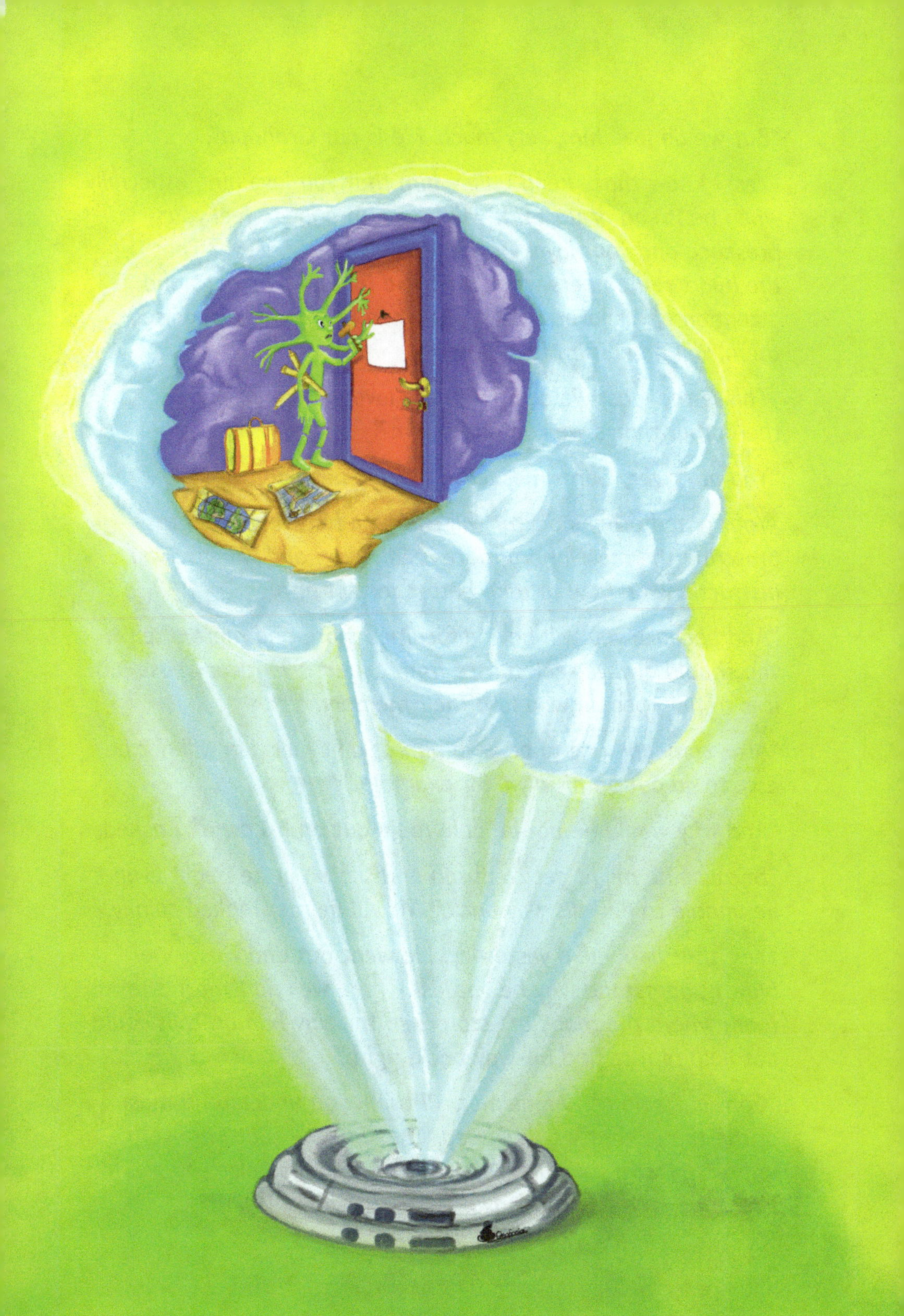

"But we do love him, very much. He is our Grandpa".

"Yes, I know that. keep telling him that you love him, especially when he is sad or upset. It will help him a lot to feel your presence and your love. Do you know what I believe? That the heart remembers what the mind forgets. The hugs and attention of his loved ones, even when he cannot recognise them, will make him feel better."

"This is the least we can do! But is love enough or are thereother things we can do for him?"

"You are right, Gerasimos. Love itself is not enough.

"Your grandfather's doctor will examine him very often to prescribe the most appropriate medication and will give you instructions on how to take better care of him.

"And because you will have difficulties more and more often, you should always seek advice from expert scientists whose job it is to help people who lose their memory.

"Also, someone has to be with him at all times. He will not be able to go out on his own, for example."

"And why would he not be able to go out on his own?" I asked.

"Because he might get confused and scared or he might even be unable to find his way back," Mr. Alzheimer replied calmly.

"Yes, that happened yesterday. He went out and was gone. Now I understand why he got lost. There was no light in the room where the maps are stored, so the tiny human cells could not help him to find his way back, right?"

"Correct," said Mr. Alzheimer. "I think you understand most of the things that we discussed. I have to say that I am very impressed with your progress. Is there anything else you would like to ask me before I leave?"

"Where are you going? I thought that you would teach me more things that I need to know."

"I think we have talked enough. The sun is about to rise and you need to wake up for school. If you think carefully about everything that we discussed, I am sure that you will find a way to help your grandfather."

"Yes, I think I understand now," I said. "I will explain everything to my Grandma and I hope she will feel better; yesterday she was crying all day."

"Oh! I shouldn't forget to tell you the most important thing of all: your Grandma will need your help."

"But our Grandma is strong and healthy, and as you said, Grandpa's disease is not infectious," I wondered. "Why should Grandma then need any help from us?"

"Yes, that's exactly what I said. But most of all, Grandma is the person who will take care of your Grandpa. She will become more and more tired and saddened by seeing him in this situation. That is why you should keep her company whenever you have some free time; it will help her to relax and feel good. This is the greatest support you can offer her."

"Be sure of this, I promise. , and besides, we always have fun with her. We will do anything that we can to help her."

"Well, I've told you everything that you will need from now on and it's time for me to go. If you need anything else, ask, search, read and learn. It's the only way to understand," said Mr. Alzheimer, and he disappeared as suddenly as he had appeared in the beginning.

I was left alone, trying to figure out the meaning of everything that Mr. Alzheimer had shown me. I looked around. Hundreds of lights were blinking. Tiny human cells were working and carrying messages. Some of them were fading away and could not work.

They certainly needed help. But from whom? I realised the difficulty and importance of the work of scientists. They research, study, and try to find out what is going on inside the brain so that they can find the cure for all those who lose their memory.

While I was deep in thought and without even feeling it coming, I suddenly opened my eyes.

I was no longer in the brain. The dream was gone. And you know, Grandpa, I think I just figured out what we need to do. The moment it will be impossible for you to stand up and walk, when it will be difficult for you to eat and drink, when you will not recognise us anymore, then we will know that most of the lights in the buildings of your brain have been destroyed. But even then, we will love you a lot because you are our beloved Grandpa! We will sit next to you, we will hold your hand, help you comb your hair, put on your cologne that you like so much; we'll keep you company as you eat your food and we will tell you stories and sing songs so you do not feel alone. You will never be alone Grandpa; you will always have us. We will take care of you and we will love you. And every night we will pray to God to finally send the cure for this strange illness so you will be with us for many years.

PS: I know that you may not understand everything that I'm writing, but I am sure you understand how much I love you, because every time I hug you, you smile happily.

I love you very, very, very much,

Your grandson,

Gerasimos.